THE NATIVITY

The Nativity

Mary Remembers

By Laurie Knowlton

Illustrated by Kasi Kubiak

Boyds Mills Press

Text copyright © 1998 by Laurie Knowlton
Illustrations copyright © 1998 by Kasi Kubiak

Published by Caroline House
Boyds Mills Press, Inc.
A Highlights Company
815 Church Street
Honesdale, Pennsylvania 18431
Printed in Mexico

Publisher Cataloging-in-Publication Data
The nativity : Mary remembers / Kasi Kubiak—1st.ed.
[32]p. : col. ill. ; cm.
Summary: The story of the first Christmas as told by Mary.
ISBN 1-56397-714-1
1. Jesus Christ—Nativity—Juvenile literature. 2. Nativity—Juvenile literature. 3. Bible stories—N.T.—Juvenile literature. [1. Jesus
Christ—Nativity. 2. Nativity. 3. Bible stories—N.T.] I. Title.
23292 / 21 —dc21   1998   AC   CIP
Library of Congress Catalog Card Number 97-77913

First edition, 1998
Book designed by Tim Gillner and Kasi Kubiak
The text of this book is set in 14-point Hiroshige Book.
The illustrations are acrylics.

10 9 8 7 6 5 4 3 2 1

God sent his messenger, the angel Gabriel, to me,
a young Nazarene woman.
I had been raised according to the law of Moses.
Long had my people prayed for the coming of the Messiah.
Now this is how his coming was foretold to me.

On an evening when I was sweeping the outer room
came a rush of wind
and a light as bright as a thousand candles.
I looked into the face of the angel Gabriel.
"Hail, Mary! The Lord is with you!"
I was bewildered by his words.
But the angel told me, "Do not be afraid.
Blessed are you among women.
God has chosen you to bear his son.
And you will call the child Jesus."

I wondered how this could be so.
I was then only engaged to Joseph.
The angel answered, "Trust that God can do all things.
The child to be born will be called holy, the Son of God."

When the angel disappeared I looked around me.
Everything in the room was the same, only I was different.
I was the servant of the Lord.
Joseph, ever faithful, also trusted in the Lord,
and took me as his wife.

As my time drew near,
the emperor Caesar Augustus ordered
that all people should return to the home
of their ancestors to be taxed and counted.

Joseph and I traveled across the desert
and up the Judean hills.
We headed for Bethlehem.
We traveled by night to avoid the scorching heat.
Joseph worried about me so.
But I trusted the angel Gabriel,
who had told me not to be afraid.

Bethlehem was filled with more people
than I had ever seen.
They packed the streets,
and crowded the inns,
and huddled in doorways.
When Joseph and I found no room,
we took shelter in a stable.
Dear Joseph, I saw the dismay written on his face.
But there was a fresh bed of hay.
And we were alone.
I was content with the stable,
and reassured Joseph that all would be well.

That night, among the animals, Jesus was born.
I wrapped him in cloth,
and made a bed in a manger filled with hay.
He held my finger in his small hand,
and I whispered, "You are the Messiah."
My soul was filled with wonder
at this blessed miracle.

Not long after the birth of Jesus,
Shepherds came to the stable.
They had been in the hills watching over their flocks
when the silence of the night was filled
with the glory of God.
An angel had appeared to them with joyful news:
"Tonight in Bethlehem the Savior is born!
He is the Anointed One!
He is Christ the Lord!
You will find the baby wrapped in cloth
and cradled in a manger."

Then the night sky shimmered
like a sparkling pond,
aglow with more angels than stars.
Praising God they said,
"Glory to God in the highest,
and peace to men of good will."

The shepherds had found my son
just as the angel had told them.
They bowed before Jesus and worshipped him.
Wondrous things had those shepherds seen that night.
"Let us go and tell the people
the Messiah has come!" they said,
and they left the stable praising God.
I held their words like a treasure in my heart.

I remember asking Joseph if he had seen the night sky.
The stars looked as if they were dancing in celebration.
Joseph smiled and told me to come and get some rest.
He was worried I would catch a chill.

I was not the only one watching the stars that night.
Three men of great wealth and wisdom
had traveled from the East following a blazing star.
The star had announced the birth of a child
born king of the Jews.
The men had stopped in Jerusalem
to ask King Herod where they might find the child.
Herod knew nothing of us.
But he asked the men to return to him
after they found the child
so that he too could honor the newborn king.

The three men continued their search
through Jerusalem
and on to Bethlehem,
where the star came to rest over our stable.

I was singing to Jesus when they appeared,
the grandest men I had ever set eyes upon.
"We have found him," said the first.
"The child born king of the Jews," said the second.
"Today we have looked into the face
of the Messiah," said the third.

The men gathered around Jesus
then fell to their knees in homage,
saying words in a language I didn't understand.
But I knew they were praising God.
They had brought gifts of gold,
frankincense, and myrrh for Jesus,
gifts for a king.
Their faces were filled with peace when they left us.
God be praised, they did not return to Herod,
but found another way home.

That night
I fell asleep
in awe of God's marvelous ways.

But sleep did not last long.
Joseph woke me and urged me to gather my things.
An angel had appeared to him in a dream
and told him that we must flee to Egypt.
Herod would try to kill my child,
because the men from the East had said
he was the newborn king of the Jews.

Fear gripped my heart as we slipped through the night.
God was sending us to Egypt.
The land that once held my people captive
would now shield his son from the sword of Herod.

Jesus slept on my shoulder.
I could feel his breath on my neck
as the donkey carried us over the sands.
The hand of the child of God reached out
and touched my face.
A feeling of peace came over me.
And though the desert was vast
and our journey long,
I knew we were not alone.

God was with us.

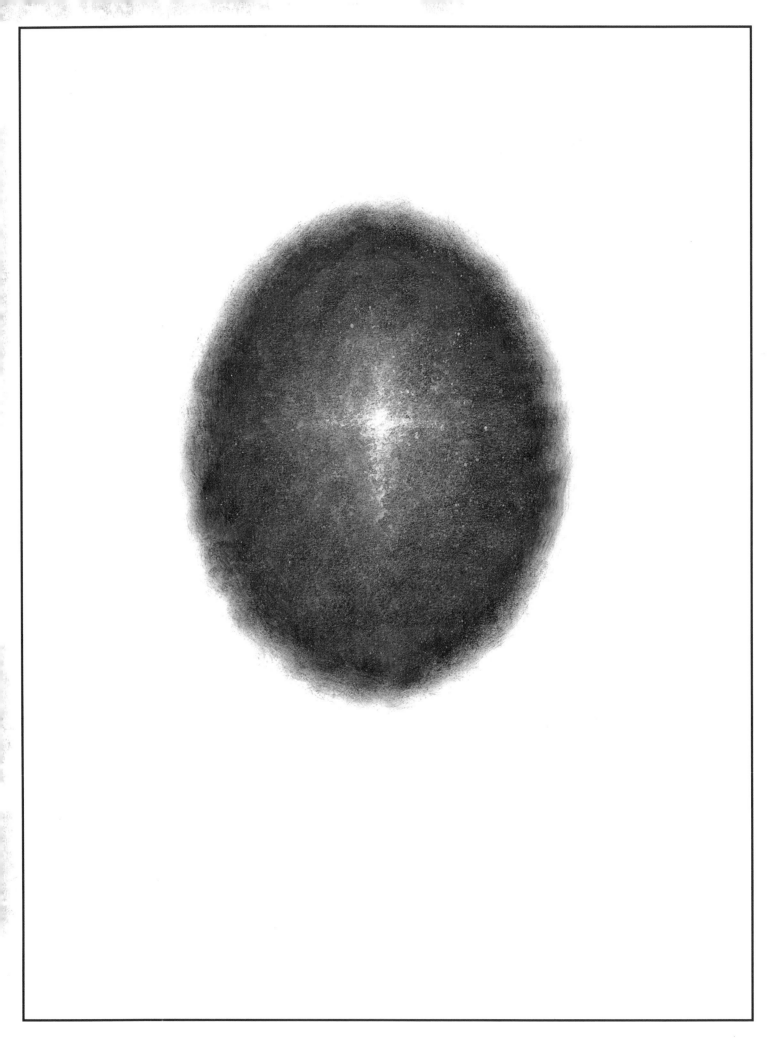